Artama
& The Watchtower Portal

The Second Journey

Bruce Paul

Artama
&
The Watchtower Portal
The Second Journey

brucepaul.com

Design by Hayes Productions
hayesproductions.com

Printed in the United States of America

Second Edition
ISBN 978-1793957191

"Bruce Paul's young adult epic fantasy, *Artama & The Watchtower Portal: The Second Journey*, is filled with color, sound, and magic . . . ."

". . . Feels authentic, aged, and with just the right touch of mystical edge."

". . . Truly a one-of-a-kind, enchanting YA fantasy . . . brought together through a flawless and poetic writing style . . . ."

". . . The author creates layers of meaning everywhere . . . ."

". . . A must-read for those who love fantasy, whether young or old."

Readers' Favorite Five-Star Award

Acknowledgements

Jim Cunningham

Lyn Hayes

David A. Lisle

Linda Mattingly

Leo Sack

Ryan Schuerger

LONG AGO, The Artama Legend began with a simple parable, *The Book of Knowledge & Wisdom*. That parable is included in this volume.

The Book of Knowledge & Wisdom

IN THE MEETING HALL, in The Town, near The Plain, in the land where the people were almost always content, the men of The Town were gathered, meeting for The Reading.

At the front of The Hall, at a large table made of the wood of the weebon tree, three old men were seated importantly. These were The Readers.

Crowding The Hall were the other men, both young and old, who gathered at the appointed hour to listen to The Reading.

The Readers read from *The Book of Knowledge &
Wisdom.*

The Book of Knowledge & Wisdom was bound in
dark leather, and the pages were edged in gold.
The pages held many words, and because there
were so many words, the words were written in
tiny letters, and The Readers used a reading glass
to see what they were reading.

The First Reader, The Honorable First Reader,
was someone splendid to behold. He wore a
reading robe as white as the full moon on a clear
night, and he wore a noble hat of stars.

The Second Reader, The Honorable Second
Reader, wore a reading robe as black as a closed
closet, and he was very fat.

The Third Reader, The Lord Most Honorable High Reader, wore a reading robe as golden as the autumn sun. And his beard was silver.

The Lord Most Honorable High Reader always read the most important words.

Near the table, an old blind man sat with his son. The First Reader read:

> Where the sun rises—as the yeast in bread—
> We call East.
> Where the sun sets—for a night of rest—
> We call West.

And the other men, both young and old, responded, "It is written. It is true."

The Second Reader read:

> When you are lost—and cannot decide—
> Let the needlebox be your guide.

The needlebox always points the way home.

And the other men recited, "It is written. It is true."

There was a pause, and then The Third Reader, The Lord Most Honorable High Reader, read the most important words:

Do not try to cross The Plain.

There is no path—or food or water—

Only dragon-fire—and dragon-slaughter.

And the other men chanted, "It is written. It is true."

The old blind man, however, did not speak, and his son noted this.

Into the night, The Reading continued, in The Meeting Hall, in The Town, near The Plain, in the land where the people were almost always content.

THE NEXT MORNING, the old blind man was in his workshop, working.

His son, Artama, was looking out the window, daydreaming.

His father made pottery from the clay from the riverbank on the edge of The Plain.

Artama painted colorful patterns on his father's work.

This morning, Artama was looking toward the east, looking toward the horizon—where the sky met The Plain.

He was not content.

Artama turned toward his father and said, "I do not see dragon-fire. I see only the blue sky and the dust of The Plain."

His father replied, "My son, I have not seen the blue sky—or the dust of The Plain—since before you were born, but I remember the beauty. If I could only see those colors again—and the colorful patterns you paint on the pottery."

His son spoke, "I want to see for myself what is across The Plain."

His father replied, "My son, when I was young, digging the clay for *my* father from the riverbank on the edge of The Plain, I too allowed my thoughts to wander—and how I wanted to follow my wandering thoughts—but there was a great need for me to stay and work. We were poor. Here I stayed. Now, I am old and blind."

The old man sighed, and then he continued, "You are young. You are strong. We are not poor. You are not bound by the need which kept me here."

Artama walked toward his father.

"But—without me—how will you see?"

"Do not be troubled, my son. I know our workshop—and the rooms of our cottage—very well." And then, his father added, "I am old, and if I travel afar, it will be in your heart. I am blind, and if I see the far edge of The Plain, it will be through your eyes."

Tears filled the eyes of both.

THE NEXT MORNING, Artama began his
journey to cross The Plain. He carried a leather
pack containing water, food, a tinderbox, and a
needlebox. He wore a blanket as a cape.

Artama turned and looked back to the
workshop.

His father was waving farewell.

Artama did not wave in return.

He walked east, onto The Plain, toward the
dawn, toward the horizon—toward the unknown.

THE DAYS WERE HOT, and the nights were cold. And the weebon trees were scarce.

The first night, the full moon was as white as The First Reader's robe. Stars were bright everywhere—a noble hat.

The second night was beyond understanding. There were no clouds. There was no moon. And there were no stars. Beyond the dimming firelight, everything disappeared—as black as The Second Reader's robe—as black as a closed closet.

Artama was thirsty and hungry and tired.

He was lost.

The words of The First Reader came into his mind:

> *Where the sun rises—as the yeast in bread—*
>
> *We call East.*
>
> *Where the sun sets—for a night of rest—*
>
> *We call West.*

But there was no sun.

Artama remembered the words of The Second Reader:

> *When you are lost—and cannot decide—*
>
> *Let the needlebox be your guide.*
>
> *The needlebox always points the way home.*

In the last light of the embers, he saw his pack. He gathered it to him and felt inside. He found the needlebox and set it on a flat stone near the dying fire.

The needlebox always points the way home.

Artama recalled the words of The Third Reader, the most important words:

> *Do not try to cross The Plain.*
>
> *There is no path—or food or water—*
>
> *Only dragon-fire—and dragon-slaughter.*

Artama knew he could turn back now.

Then, he remembered the words of his father: *"I am old, and if I travel afar, it will be in your heart. I am blind, and if I see the far edge of The Plain, it will be through your eyes."*

Artama stared into the embers, and he saw the point of no return.

He tightened his blanket around his shoulders.

Artama knew he must continue . . . .

THERE WAS A FLASH of blue and gold and white.

When he awoke, it felt like a dream.

Artama was looking out a window. The sky was blue—azure. In the sunlight, there was a garden and a lawn and a golden fountain. Children were playing.

Artama could hear them speak, but he could not understand their words.

At the golden fountain, a girl was filling a jar

with water. The water was silver in the sunlight.

When the jar was full, she stood and walked away, out of sight.

Artama looked at his clothes. They were the style worn by the children in the garden.

He looked around the room.

He saw his pack on a table. Next to his pack was a cup. And next to the cup was a scarf, neatly folded.

He heard a knock at the door.

A moment passed.

The door opened.

It was the girl.

She was holding the jar.

"I am Kora," she said, smiling. "I brought you water . . . from the golden fountain."

Artama was smiling too. He looked out the window to the garden and the lawn and the golden fountain. He looked again to Kora. "I am Artama."

He paused—bewildered—and then he continued, "Unlike the others, you speak in my words."

Kora said, "I speak in your words, so you will understand."

"Where am I?"

"Across The Plain."

ARTAMA TOLD KORA about crossing The Plain. He tried to tell her about the blackness, about being lost.

She nodded. "I know. I had a dream . . . a vision . . . I could *see*."

Kora poured water from the jar into the cup and gave it to him. "Drink. It will give you strength."

Then she unfolded the scarf, spreading it on the table. The fabric was beautiful . . . unknown.

In the center of the scarf was a nutshell. Kora lifted the top, revealing a glowing amber ointment. "When you return, apply this to your father's eyes. He will see. They will *all* see."

"I have many questions."

"I know."

"How am I here?"

"It is a matter of the heart."

Into the night, Artama and Kora talked about matters of the heart, and Artama asked many questions.

THERE WAS A FLASH of blue and gold and white.

When he awoke, it felt like a dream.

The sun was golden, like autumn, like the robe of The Third Reader, The Lord Most Honorable High Reader.

Artama looked at his clothes, and he saw the clothes of his dream.

He saw his pack.

He saw the needlebox, still on the flat stone,

pointing the way home.

He reached inside his pack and found the scarf.

On the ground, he unfolded it. The nutshell was there. He carefully opened it. The amber ointment glowed.

He closed the nutshell, folded the scarf around it, and put it back in his pack. He picked up the needlebox.

Heading for home, the earth moved beneath his feet.

IN THE DOORWAY of The Meeting Hall, in The Town, near The Plain, in the land where the people were almost always content, Artama stood quietly, listening to The Reading.

The First Reader read from *The Book of Knowledge & Wisdom*:

> Where the sun rises—as the yeast in bread—
> We call East.
> Where the sun sets—for a night of rest—
> We call West.

And the other men, both young and old, responded, "It is written. It is true."

Artama saw his father at the front of The Hall. The Second Reader read:

When you are lost—and cannot decide—

Let the needlebox be your guide.

The needlebox always points the way home.

And the other men recited, "It is written. It is true."

There was a pause. And then, The Third Reader, The Lord Most Honorable High Reader, read:

Do not try to cross The Plain.

There is no path—or food or water—

Only dragon-fire—and dragon-slaughter.

And the other men chanted, "It is written. It is true."

Artama stepped forward. "It is *not* true!"

Everyone in The Hall turned to look at him.

He exclaimed, "Although it is written, it is *not* true!"

Everyone was silent.

"I have crossed The Plain, and I have returned. I saw no dragon-fire. I saw no dragon-slaughter. Truly, it is a beautiful place."

The First Reader, The Reader in white, put his hand on his noble hat.

The Second Reader, The Reader in black, puffed his cheeks and looked very fat.

The Third Reader, The Reader in gold, ran his fingers through his silver beard.

The old blind man shouted with joy, "My son!"

Artama ran to the front of The Hall and

embraced his father. "I have crossed The Plain and returned!"

The Reader in black shouted, "Silence!"

Artama looked at him. "I will *not* be silent. I have crossed The Plain and returned."

The Reader in black shouted, "No one has ever crossed The Plain and returned!"

"Look at my clothes. These are not the clothes of The Town. This fabric is unknown."

Artama described the blackness . . . and the garden and the lawn and the golden fountain. He told them about the girl—Kora—and the silver water in the sunlight . . . and the nutshell.

"The nutshell!"

Artama reached inside his pack and withdrew the scarf. He unfolded it. In the center was the nutshell. He carefully lifted the top. The amber ointment glowed.

He touched it with his finger.

Then, he touched his father's eyes.

His father squinted and looked around the room.

Then, he laughed and shouted, "I can see! I can see!"

Everyone in The Hall gasped.

The First Reader put his hand on his hat.

The Second Reader puffed his cheeks.

The Third Reader, The Lord Most Honorable High Reader, ran his fingers through his beard.

And then he looked at the old man and said, "Describe your son's clothing."

The father described his son's clothing in

perfect detail.

The Lord Most Honorable High Reader looked at the boy who had crossed The Plain and returned—and at the old blind man who could now see—and he spoke, "Young man, Artama, you are blessed. You have shown great courage, and you are wise beyond your years."

The Lord Most Honorable High Reader paused . . . and then he continued, "You shall be The Writer. You shall write words of knowledge and wisdom in *The Book of Knowledge & Wisdom*. Take this pen and write."

Artama took the pen.

The Hall was silent.

Artama turned to the first page in *The Book of Knowledge & Wisdom*, and he wrote:

Some of what is
written is true.

Artama
& The Watchtower Portal

The Second Journey

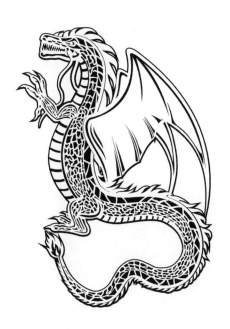

1

IN THE LAND where the people were almost always content, near The Plain, in The Town, in the cottage, in the workshop, at his reading table near the window, Artama was reading. Now that he was The Writer—and wrote in *The Book of Knowledge & Wisdom*—he read more than ever. Artama enjoyed reading.

His father was painting. Now that he could see again, he painted again. He painted patterns on the pottery that Artama made from the clay from the riverbank on the edge of The Plain. He was painting the head of a dragon with a roaring open mouth, and streaming from the open mouth, he painted a long red tongue of dragon-fire—a storming red swirl into a red sky.

Artama looked up from his book. The late–afternoon golden sunlight was glowing through the window. The reading table was stacked with books.

Artama poured water from a pitcher into a cup. Before he crossed The Plain—when his father was blind— Artama had painted the patterns on both pieces of pottery. Now, he noted the bubbles on the water in the cup. For a moment they appeared, tended to gather and merge, and at last, they burst—becoming one with the air.

On one of the stacks of books, near the window, was a bowl filled with weebons—the red fruit of the weebon tree. Artama noted a weeworm crawling from one weebon to another—in the bowl, on the stack of books, on the table, near the window, in the workshop . . . in the cottage . . . in The Town . . . near The Plain . . . in the land where the people were almost always content . . . .

Artama smiled. He looked toward his father. Artama was content.

There was a loud knock on the door, followed by an

urgent cry: "Artama! Artama!"

His father dipped his brush into the red paint.

Artama went quickly to the door.

His father painted a storming red swirl into a red sky—a long red tongue of dragon-fire.

Artama opened the door. The runner of The Town stood there, breathless. Artama knew him well. "Taladar!"

"The Readers sent me! You must come to The Hall, at once!"

"Why?"

"I know only this: They are looking for you."

"*Who* is looking for me?"

Taladar shuddered. "An unholy horde, an evil army." He wiped his mouth with the back of his hand to clean away the words. "A man from The West is talking with The Readers now. He escaped, and he came to warn us."

"Why *me*?" But Artama already knew.

Taladar shuddered again. He hesitated. "Because you know the way across The Plain. They think you can lead them to gold."

Artama understood. He motioned to his father. His father understood.

Today was the day it had to be.

Into the late-afternoon golden sunlight, Artama ran down familiar streets, through The Town, toward The Hall. He ran, and his thoughts raced.

The earth moved beneath his feet.

Artama thought about his father's paintings and about crossing The Plain. He thought about Kora—the wondrous girl across The Plain, the girl who cared for him, who gave him water from the golden fountain for his journey home, who gave him the amber ointment for his father's eyes, who talked with him into the night about matters of the heart.

The late-afternoon sunlight began turning red.

Among the buildings in The Town, the streets were empty.

Dogs barked, and cats ran.

All of the people—the men, the women, the children—

were gathered at The Hall.

To The West, the land rose steeply in waves of grass, and the horizon was near. The sky was glowing a deepening red.

The crowd babbled.

Through the doorway of The Hall, the crowd pressed forward to the reading table where The Readers were debating.

The First Reader, The Reader in white, adjusted his noble hat.

The Second Reader, The Reader in black, puffed his cheeks and looked very fat. He pointed to a passage in *The Book of Knowledge & Wisdom*.

The Third Reader, The Reader in gold—The Lord Most Honorable High Reader—leaned forward and silently read:

> Do not try to cross The Plain.
>
> There is no path—or food or water—
>
> Only dragon-fire—and dragon-slaughter.

At the end of the table, the man from The West stood

with his back to a window that opened to the red sky. The man was battered and dirty. His lips were cracked and swollen. He looked over his shoulder frequently.

As Artama approached The Hall, he could hear the crowd. He thought about the storming red swirl into the red sky, and he thought about crossing The Plain . . . and he thought about Kora. In his mind, he heard voices, voices that were pure. The harmony resonated and reverberated . . . . He could not recognize the voices, nor could he understand them. But he understood, nonetheless. He felt far away, far away from everything—except the voices.

As Artama walked through the doorway of The Hall, the people stepped back.

The Lord Most Honorable High Reader looked up from *The Book of Knowledge & Wisdom.*

Their eyes met.

"Artama! Quickly!" he beckoned.

Artama went quickly to the front of The Hall.

Children were crying.

In his mind, Artama could see the colors of the chorus,

the pure voices, the song everlasting, beyond the blue and gold and white. And he saw blood swirling in the air—bright red—*his* blood.

Artama stood at the table.

The Reader in black commanded the man from The West, "Tell him!"

"I escaped from my town. They burned it down. They are looking for *you*."

"Why are they looking for *me*?" But Artama already knew.

"Because you know the way across The Plain. The news has traveled far. In all the land, the people tell the tale of Artama: Artama slew dragons and found gold—treasures beyond imagination."

Artama raised his hand. "I never—"

"These men want gold!" shouted the man from The West. "They are dragons. They seek *only* gold. If they cannot find gold, they *will* take blood. They bring only unholy fire."

"Dragons?"

"They are men, but their banner is the head of a dragon with a roaring open mouth—"

"*You* brought this upon us!" shouted The Reader in black, pointing at Artama. The Reader's face was red with rage. He quoted vehemently from *The Book of Knowledge & Wisdom*:

> Do not try to cross The Plain.
>
> There is no path—or food or water—
>
> Only dragon-fire—and dragon-slaughter.

The man from The West continued hopelessly, "They thought you lived in our town. When they learned otherwise, they lined the men along a wall and began beheading them. The first man lost his head. The second man as well. The third man, an old man, told them where you lived. But it did not matter. With flaming arrows, they set my town on fire. They burned my home! They burned my family! They will have only gold—or blood. They take joy in ungodly fire."

The Reader in black shouted again, "Look what you have brought upon us!"

"This is all *your* fault, Artama!" echoed some in the crowd.

"Artama, help us!" cried others.

The Lord Most Honorable High Reader raised his hand.

The Hall fell silent.

Artama spoke, "I have a plan." He paused. "I will agree to lead them onto The Plain, and I will lead them away."

The First Reader said, "But if you lead them across The Plain, when they find what they want, they will plunder and waste. They will bring ruin, and they will kill you— they will need you no longer."

"I can lead them *onto* The Plain. But I will not lead them *across* it." For Artama knew he could not: To journey across The Plain is a matter of the heart.

"But if they do not find what they want, they will surely kill you," said The Reader in white.

A wry smile came to the face of The Reader in black.

Outside, a man shouted, "Look!" There was a collective gasp from the crowd, and then the crowd grew louder, and the sound moved as a wave through the doorway.

Inside, the crowd pressed toward the windows to see.

On the horizon, a dirty cloud of storming red dust was rising.

A woman at a window screamed.

Appearing over the horizon—slowly—was a head of a dragon, a banner with a roaring open mouth, and streaming from the open mouth was the long red tongue of dragon-fire—the storming red swirl into the red sky. In the wind, the banner looked alive against the dying sun.

A horseman on a huge gray horse held the banner high. And then he jammed the staff into the ground. On either side, a horseman rode up and stopped, each with a bow ready to shoot a flaming arrow. The dragon-tongue snapped in the wind. The horses reared. Each bowman shot his flaming arrow into a steep, high arc—one off to the left, one off to the right.

There were screams from the crowd.

When the arrows hit the ground, each became a tower of flame.

The Hall was chaos. Children were crying, and women were trying to comfort them. Men pushed to the windows.

Over the horizon, on a huge black horse, a dark sinister figure appeared, his black cape flowing. He rode to the banner and stopped.

The Hall fell silent again.

The Reader in black turned toward Artama and shouted, "Go! Now! Lead them away!"

The Reader in white said reverently, "Artama, you shall be remembered in story and song. Volumes shall be written about you."

The Reader in gold, The Lord Most Honorable High Reader, solemnly concluded, "Artama, I pray for you."

Artama's father was in the doorway of The Hall. Taladar was at his side. Artama's father stepped forward and made his way toward his son. He was carrying a blanket and a leather pack.

Artama walked to him.

His father gave him the blanket and the pack. "The needlebox is inside."

"Father, pray I am right."

"My son, I pray."

Artama found himself walking through the crowd, toward the darkening red horizon. Things had never looked so clear. The air was clean. Everything was crystal at the edge. Artama was in the moment . . . in the middle of eternity. He had no sense of fear. He had no sense of time. He was . . . *there.* Floating in the center of infinity. Immortal.

The ground rose steeply before him. As he walked, he felt around in the pack until he found the needlebox. He stopped and turned away from the horizon, as though looking back. He removed the needlebox from the pack and slipped it into his pocket. He turned back toward the horizon and started walking again.

Silhouetted against the dark red sky, between two towers of flame—on his huge black warhorse—the commander of the horde watched Artama approach.

The commander raised a magnificent sword, extravagantly decorated with gold, high above his head.

There was an oily stench in the air. Heavy gold chains—gaudy, mismatched, and chaotic—tangled, twisted, and knotted—hung around his neck. His face was disfigured by a terrible scar—a scar from fire—down his left temple and cheek. His left eye was partially closed by the damage.

Now, Artama was standing before him. "I am Artama."

"*I* am Zortan!" He pounded his chest with his left fist. The huge black destrier shifted. "I have been looking for you."

"I know," said Artama resignedly. He paused, and then he simply stated, "I will lead you onto The Plain, but you must spare my people and my town."

Zortan chuckled. "Tell me, *Artama*, why must I spare your people and your town?"

"As a condition."

Zortan laughed. "You are in no position to set conditions. I will do as I please. I will take your head, drink your blood, and burn your town—leaving nothing but ashes."

"Then who will lead you to your destiny?"

Zortan stopped laughing. He turned toward the men behind him and commanded, "Take him! Shackle him!"

Three men were quick to step forward. One took Artama's pack, another took his blanket, and the third roughly pushed Artama away, toward the horizon.

The sky was blood red.

Zortan proclaimed, "We will camp here tonight!"

It was dark. It was black, except for the red glow over the horizon.

That night, the people of The Town did not sleep.

In the cottages, the women comforted the children.

The men gathered in groups along the edge of The Town. They looked toward the horizon to The West. The banner, the silhouette of the head of the dragon, waved against a sinful red glow. The men carried common tools as hopeless weapons of defense: hammers and axes and shovels and rakes. Quietly, they talked. Sometimes, over the horizon, they could see the high arc of a glowing coal. They could hear shouts and laughter, and mixed among the shouts and laughter, there were cries of pain. There were curses. And then more laughter.

In The Hall, The First Reader walked away from the window, from the nightmare. He sat at the table, tore off his hat, and ran his fingers through his hair.

In The Hall, The Second Reader was puffing his cheeks, studying a passage in *The Book of Knowledge & Wisdom*.

The Third Reader was not in The Hall. His golden robe was hanging on a hook. He was walking along the edge of The Town, in common clothes, among the men, talking with them, offering encouragement.

Meanwhile, in his cottage, in the candlelight, Artama's father sat at the reading table, his hands folded and his head bowed.

Now, The Lord Most Honorable High Reader was walking into the heart of The Town, toward Artama's home.

Candles lit every dwelling along the way.

One old woman stood in the doorway of her cottage,

holding a broom.

In his cottage, in the candlelight, Artama's father lowered his head onto his hands.

There was a knock on the door, a gentle knock, followed by a simple statement: "It is I." The voice was unmistakable.

Artama's father opened the door.

The Lord Most Honorable High Reader asked, "Alagon, may I?"

Artama's father answered, "Valdar, please."

At the reading table, the two old men—the two old friends—sat and began to talk.

Alagon poured water from the pitcher into a cup and gave it to Valdar.

For a moment, bubbles appeared. They tended to gather and merge, and at last, they burst—becoming one with the air.

"I lost my sight before my son was born," Alagon began, "but I remembered the beauty, and when he talked with me about crossing The Plain, I encouraged him. I told him, when I was young, I too wanted to cross The Plain. I remember saying, 'I am old, and if I travel afar, it will be in your heart. I am blind, and if I see the far edge of The Plain, it will be through your eyes.'

"My son crossed The Plain and returned. He brought the amber ointment for my eyes, and now I can see. I see the head of a dragon with a roaring open mouth . . . . I would gladly be blind again. I would gladly go now in his place."

Valdar spoke, "We are both old, and we have seen many things. Some may say we have seen *too many* things. But what we saw today—what we saw in your son—we will never live to see again."

"I blessed him. And now, I may have lost him. He may be sacrificed."

"Would you not have gone then, as you would go now?"

Alagon nodded.

"Be proud."

"I *am* proud, Valdar, but that does not lessen my

dread."

"Artama is wise and clever. He will not be a sacrifice."

"We will see what is given."

Valdar rose and nodded to Alagon. "Now, I must return to the men."

As Valdar walked toward the edge of The Town, he passed the old woman, still standing in her doorway, holding her broom. He nodded and continued on his way.

Candles lit every dwelling.

For the people in The Town, on the edge of The Plain, in the center of infinity, the night seemed endless, in the middle of eternity.

On the eastern horizon, the black sky gradually became indigo and gradually became light. Eventually, the crown of the sun appeared, but no one noticed. All eyes were on the western horizon.

In the first light, the horseman on the gray charger rode up and pulled the banner from the ground and held it high.

Next on the horizon, Artama appeared, walking toward The Town. Zortan rode behind him. The horseman with the banner moved off to the right. Following were more horsemen. Among them were bowmen with strong arms, wearing black leather helmets with reptilian spikes down from the crown—dragon-spikes. Following them were men on foot, two or three abreast, beastly men, oily men, ungodly men, dragon-men. Next, came the wagons drawn by horses, carrying supplies: barrels of water and weebon wine, crates of food, and weapons. Then came the wagon carrying fire-oil. Chained to it was an old man, a prisoner, struggling to keep on his feet. The last wagon carried The Fire. The Fireman guarded it jealously. The last horseman, a bowman, was the last guard: The Last Man.

Only the dogs ran free.

The Lord Most Honorable High Reader turned to Taladar, "Go! Tell Alagon!"

The golden morning sunlight was gleaming in Artama's eyes, as he walked toward The Town. Gradually, he began turning, curving off to the right, walking south, leading Zortan away.

The dogs followed.

There was a loud knock on the door. Alagon moved as quickly as he could to open it.

"Artama is alive!" Taladar exclaimed. "And he is leading them away!"

Together, Alagon and Taladar made their way through The Town again, this time toward the southern edge. They arrived to see Artama turning east, leading the dragon-men toward the rising sun, onto The Plain, away from The Town.

Dust filled the air.

The men of The Town watched.

Gradually, women and children began to join the men, and they all watched as Artama led the horde away.

Artama disappeared first—over the horizon—followed by Zortan, the dragon-banner, the horsemen, the beastly men, the wagon of oil, the old man, the wagon of The Fire, The Fireman, and The Last Man.

The dogs followed.

Among the people of The Town nothing was said. Eventually, they turned away . . . silently returning to their lives.

2

OVER THE HORIZON, on The Plain, the vastness was endless. The colors were magnificent—few but splendid. The sky was azure, and the sun glowed above the pastel dust. In the distance, there were rocks and spires and towers of rock . . . and few weebon trees.

In the warmth of the rising sun, a chill came over Artama, and a shiver crossed his shoulders. Everywhere was the same: endless pastel dust.

Artama led the way, and he knew he was lost.

Zortan followed.

Artama's young bones felt old . . . and cold. Last night, his sleep was fitful. He had no blanket, and the blackness was immitigably cold. All through the night, he heard the laughter and the curses and the cries of the beastly men.

The guards had shackled him to a rusting chain staked into the ground, and he could take only five strides in any direction. He could not see what he could hear. Zortan's tent blocked his view. He could, however, see the old man—the prisoner—shackled to another rusting chain staked into the ground. Artama wondered about him. Artama wondered about his father and The Readers and The Town . . . and Kora . . . across The Plain. In his mind, Artama heard voices—singing—voices that were pure. The harmony resonated and reverberated . . . .

This morning, on The Plain, there was only one satisfaction: With every step he took, Artama took Zortan and the beastly men a step farther away from The Town, away from his home.

Artama continued walking east.

The ungodly men were tired from the night: too much drinking and too little sleep, too much of The Game—wagering on everything. They complained loudly among themselves. Zortan's horsemen rode around them, keeping them in order by force—by curses—and by promises of gold.

In time, as the sun warmed the unholy men, their mood improved, and they began singing a marching song:

We don't fear dragons,

And we don't fear men.

We carry The Fire in a wagon.

Some of us are young,

And some of us are old,

And every one of us

Will drink your blood and take your gold.

We march in the morning.

At night we drink and parlay.

We don't care about yesterday.

And the men continued marching onto The Plain, into the heat of the day, into the dust.

That night, it was cold again. The full moon was as white as The First Reader's robe. Stars were bright everywhere.

Artama asked for his blanket.

"We gave your blanket to the dogs," the guard barked.

"Tell Zortan I need a blanket."

The guard turned his back and walked away haughtily, toward Zortan's tent.

That night, Artama saw The Game for the first time. He could walk to the end of the chain and see beyond Zortan's tent. He could see a circle of beastly men. And in the center of the circle was a young man wearing a black leather helmet with reptilian spikes—dragon-spikes—running down from the crown. He wore black leather gloves, and he crouched beside a blazing fire—red and orange and yellow. The Point. A dirty black cloud boiled into the night.

The beastly men in the circle fiercely threw glowing coals at the young man, and he batted them away—or caught them and threw them back in his own attack. The Fireman made his way furiously around the circle, carrying pots of glowing coals to the men who paid him well in gold. Gold coins, gold chains, and gold rings changed hands constantly. The beastly men wagered on everything.

Artama shivered. He looked over to the shackled old man.

Their eyes met, but the old man looked away.

"Are you enjoying The Game?" asked Zortan, now standing by Artama.

The guard stood a few paces away.

"It looks pointless."

Zortan laughed. "But, Artama, *wise* Artama, the man in the center *is* The Point. It is about gold. It is *all* about gold. Surely, someone of your understanding understands this." Zortan turned to the guard and commanded, "Bring him his blanket."

The guard walked away subserviently.

"Someday, Artama, *you* will be The Point—unless you lead me across The Plain."

Artama watched the circle of men fiercely throwing glowing coals.

Constantly, gold coins, gold chains, and gold rings changed hands.

Zortan walked away toward his tent, not saying another word.

The guard returned and threw Artama his blanket disdainfully.

Artama eagerly wrapped it around his shoulders. He could smell the dogs.

At last, on the cold ground, Artama fell into an uneasy sleep. He dreamed of dragons . . . reptilian spikes . . . the beastly men . . . and a terrible fire. He saw a circle of fiery dragons, and in the center, he saw a storming red swirl into a red sky . . . .

Meanwhile, in The Game, in the center of the circle, the young man was hit in the face and knocked to the ground. Glowing coals showered down from high arcs. Gold coins, gold chains, and gold rings changed hands. The men laughed and cursed.

Artama awoke abruptly.

He tightened his blanket around his shoulders and

watched The Game again, until he fell asleep again . . . dreaming of dragons and the storming red swirl into the red sky.

In the morning, Artama led the way. Dust blew in his face as he squinted into the rising sun. He felt for the needlebox in his pocket. If Zortan ever discovered it, he would find The Town and burn it. Artama turned his back to the wind. He squinted down the line of the horde: Zortan, the dragon-banner, the horsemen, the beastly men, the wagons of food and water and weapons and weebon wine, the wagon of oil, the old man, the wagon of The Fire, The Fireman, The Last Man . . . and the dogs.

Now, the weebon trees were scarce. Rocks were scattered everywhere, and the dust blew viciously.

Some dogs barked, and some dogs whined.

Artama recalled the late-afternoon golden sunlight glowing in the window . . . the reading table stacked with books . . . the weeworm crawling from one sphere to another . . . and the bubbles on the water in the cup.

He shivered.

The beastly men were rancorous. In an effort to distract them, one of the horsemen began shouting—singing in a loud, coarse voice through the vicious dust:

> Tonight, I'll burn you in The Game.
>
> I don't fear your fiery throws.
>
> I can dance with the flames.
>
> I'll take your gold . . .
>
> And bury you in coals.

And the men continued marching onto The Plain, into dust.

That night was beyond understanding. There were no clouds. There was no moon. And there were no stars. Beyond the firelight, beyond the circle of the beastly men, everything disappeared into black—as black as The Second Reader's robe.

Artama watched The Game again.

In Zortan's tent a debate was raging.

Artama was thinking about his escape. He heard the

words from *The Book of Knowledge & Wisdom*:

> *When you are lost—and cannot decide—*
>
> *Let the needlebox be your guide.*
>
> *The needlebox always points the way home.*

But how could he escape the horsemen and the dogs and the arrows?

He looked away from the fire. He looked to the old man, but the old man once again turned away, avoiding Artama's eyes.

"Are you enjoying The Game tonight?" Zortan was now standing there—again.

"Who is the old man?"

Zortan chuckled. "He is the old fool who told me where you lived."

"Why not release him? He told you what you needed."

Zortan sneered. "He would die in the dust anyway. It is more powerful to have a prisoner, an enemy, someone for the men to hate. But this man has outlived his usefulness. He is old and slow. No prisoner ever rides. When he cannot walk, he dies."

And Zortan continued, but Artama was lost in a vision: The wind was overwhelming and dust was driven everywhere. The Fireman was desperately trying to save The Fire amid a storming red swirl of flames. Artama saw the end was near. The voices were pure. The harmony resonated and reverberated . . . .

The vision waned to the beastly men chanting, "Art-a-ma! Art-a-ma!"

Zortan laughed. "They want to kill you. They say, 'He's not leading us anywhere. He's taking us in circles, prolonging his life in the grasp of death.' They fear we are lost. I must give them *something*."

Artama stared into Zortan's eyes.

Zortan said, "I will spare your life, Artama, *only* if you lead me across The Plain. If not, I will give you to The Game." Zortan signaled to a guard and commanded, "Take the old man!"

"Help me! Artama!" the old man cried in terror. "Help me!"

The guard pushed the old man toward the fire.

"Help me!"

Artama was helpless.

"I curse you, Artama!" the old man screamed. "*You* brought this upon me."

The guard pushed the old man down to the circle of the beastly men and threw him into The Point.

The men roared, and the wagering began.

The Fireman ran furiously around the circle, carrying the pots of glowing coals. There were shouts and curses and laughter.

It was a matter of profit—and pride—to throw a coal in a high arc and hit The Point. But the most vicious men threw straight for the head. There was no art in their attack. Gold coins, gold chains, and gold rings changed hands.

Zortan said enticingly, "You are not common, Artama. You do not need to die. If you lead me across The Plain, I *will* reward you—I will honor you with gold." Then, he walked away, back to his tent.

Artama could soon hear a debate raging again.

He knew he could not lead them across The Plain.

Ruthlessly hit with glowing coals, the old man fell under the rain of fire. He struggled, thrashing and screaming, but he was soon buried in glowing coals. Gold coins, gold chains, and gold rings changed hands.

The smoke of burning flesh filled the air.

Artama wept.

3

THE MORNING WAS OVERCAST. The sky was dull, unpolished pewter.

Artama walked, and Zortan rode, east toward the horizon.

The Plain was unchanged: endlessly the same—endless dust, rocks, spires, and towers of rock.

To the south, there was a wall of spires, and among them, the tallest was like a watchtower. Beyond the wall of spires, beyond the watchtower of rock, the sky was turning faintly red, as though another sunrise, but a sunrise in the south. There were red pulses of light—exploding torches—deep within.

The bearer of the banner followed Artama and Zortan. His huge gray charger seemed almost silver beneath the dullness of the sky.

Then came the horsemen.

The unholy horde raggedly followed, once again burdened with the night: too much drinking and too little sleep, too much of The Game. Their lust for gold and fire and blood was pulsing. They blood-lusted for Artama at The Point. Tonight. They wanted to bury him in coals.

Dust began gently swirling in the air.

Zortan rode up to Artama and commanded, "Stop!" There was an oily stench in the air. Towering on his huge black horse, Zortan spoke, "I have debated this, and I am tired of it. I have made my decision. Today is your last chance. Unless you show me something, we are turning back in the morning. I will proclaim it at The Game tonight. Some will be angry. Some will be relieved. They will *all* enjoy seeing you at The Point."

Artama responded, "The end is near. Do you really want to turn back now?"

Zortan looked closely at Artama with his right eye.

Artama spoke adamantly, "I need to climb that tower—to see."

Zortan shook his head. The warhorse shook as well. Zortan repeated, "This is your last chance."

"I need to climb the tower."

Zortan motioned for two guards and commanded, "Take him to his tower."

One guard, wearing a dirty red shirt, carried a spear. The other guard, in a tattered black shirt, carried a sword. They roughly pushed Artama forward.

The guard in black prodded Artama with his sword.

A few steps later, the guard with the spear swept Artama's feet out from under him, and Artama fell into the dust.

The guards laughed.

Artama regained his footing and turned toward them, glaring. His face was streaked with sweat and dust, and dust and sweat were in his eyes. Tears ran down his cheeks.

The guards jeered.

The guard in black put the tip of his sword under Artama's chin, taunting him. "What're you going to do? Cry?"

The guard in the dirty red shirt scoffed, "You're a dead man walking—or should I say stumbling?"

Sarcastically, the guard in black said, "I wouldn't call him a man, but *dead*—certainly." And then he pushed Artama again. "I'll bury you in coals and hear you scream."

And so Artama and the guards made their way, haltingly, toward the tower.

The dust was swirling.

At the base of the tower, the guard in black ran the tip of his sword down the vertebrae of Artama's back.

Artama thought of Kora . . . across The Plain . . . filling the jar with water.

The guard with the spear jabbed Artama again. "Climb your tower. Take a last look."

The tower was almost straight up. There were places to hold and places to step, but they were few. The starkness was like the moon.

Looking up the side of the tower, the guard with the sword snorted, "I'll be here—waiting."

Artama began climbing. He worked carefully, hand and foot.

The sky was still gray, although brighter. To the south, it was a brighter angry red.

What could he hope for at the top of the tower?

He felt a sharp pain in his back. And then another. He could not breathe. He could hear the guards taunting him as they threw rocks.

"Just practicing!" the guard in black shouted.

Artama was now climbing for his life. He struggled to find holds and steps. A rock hit his right hand, almost costing him his grip.

And then, in the moment when Artama turned his head, a rock hit, splitting open the center of his forehead—a bursting red star of torn flesh—sending blood swirling in the air.

Artama could only endure. Beyond that, he was helpless. But if he endured, he could climb beyond the threat of the rocks, beyond the power of the guards.

At last, he reached the top of the tower and crawled over a low wall of rocks on the rim. On the other side he leaned back against the wall. Blood was running down onto his nose and cheeks. He wiped it away and wiped his bloody hand on his leg.

Finally, he was safe, and although he could hear the guards cursing, it was almost quiet.

He could think.

He considered his options. He knew Zortan might need him to die tonight. If Zortan found the needlebox, he would find The Town and burn it. He *could* tell Zortan about the needlebox. He *could* tell Zortan he would lead him back. If he did, he would have more time to escape, but when they found The Town . . . . He could save himself a while longer, but in the end, Zortan would send him to The Point to be killed. But if he could escape—somehow. How could he outrun the horsemen and the dogs and the arrows?

Artama removed the needlebox from his pocket and

set it on a flat stone. Slowly, he raised a heavy jagged rock over his head, prepared to smash the guide.

In his mind, Artama saw the late-afternoon golden sunlight glowing through the window, and he saw the reading table stacked with books. He smelled the aroma of the leather bindings and the fragrant pages, and he saw the weeworm crawling from one weebon to another . . . and the bubbles in the cup.

Then, he heard the red storm.

To the south, the sky was on fire.

Artama dropped the rock and stared in amazement. Dragons flew straight toward the tower—an undulating swarm of ancient, fire-breathing, reptilian creatures. Artama crouched among the rocks at the edge of the tower and watched as the swarm flew directly over him.

The first dragons were small, with keen red eyes. Their wings were translucent and fast—whining. These dragons were quick and agile. Smoke blew back from their nostrils and fire torched from their mouths. They had fierce talons. But their eyesight was their power.

Following the dragons with red eyes were larger dragons—dragons with yellow eyes. Their wings were thicker membranes. They too had flaming mouths. But their power was in their talons: brutal, ripping, shredding blades.

The whining became a deeper humming despair.

Then came the true dragons of fire, dragons with blue eyes—gargantuan creatures that could produce almost invisible heat.

Artama witnessed the terror.

The leading dragons—the small darting dragons—separated, some flying off to the left and some flying off to the right, and they flew in upward spirals, higher and higher.

The larger dragons flew straight toward the unholy horde.

The Last Man was attacked first.

A dragon with yellow eyes, flame torching from its mouth, set him on fire.

Another dragon with yellow eyes took the burning

Last Man in its talons and flew in an upward spiral. The Last Man was flailing and screaming. The dragon rose higher and higher . . . a storming red swirl into the red sky.

The guard in black ran.

Another dragon with yellow eyes killed him instantly—talons ripping off his head.

The Fireman, desperately trying to protect The Fire, died next. More dragons with yellow eyes and furious teeth and flaming tongues devoured him.

The guard with the spear tried to hide, but to no avail. He was set on fire and ran insanely screaming.

The dragon clutching The Last Man dropped him from high in the fiery air, and the body fell—flaming—onto the wagon carrying the fire-oil. Soon, there was a roar of flame and a boiling cloud of dirty black smoke.

The last wagon, the wagon carrying The Fire, was consumed in flames.

The living were cursing and screaming.

Black smoke was rising from the dead.

The stench was miasmic.

Some remaining bowmen launched a wave of flaming arrows toward the diving dragons . . . but the arrows were shot in vain, merely making high arcs of fire.

Repeatedly, the dragons torched the bowmen.

At last, a flaming arrow tore into the red eye of a dragon. Other bowmen saw the crippled creature and shot more arrows. Finally, one hit under its wing. The dragon swirled upward and hovered . . . and then fell and recovered, swirling upward again.

Artama saw it coming for the tower.

Flying with only one wing, the dragon rose steeply and then fell. Diving straight for the tower, the creature crashed, the first arrow protruding from its eye, the second arrow buried under its wing. The dragon clutched the rim of the tower. The undamaged eye stared straight at Artama.

Artama looked straight back.

The heat was intense.

The dragon lost its grip and fell.

Artama looked over the rim of the tower and saw

the burning beastly men scattered across The Plain. He smelled their burning flesh.

Two dragons with red eyes swooped down and attacked the horseman with the banner, their talons ripping into his shoulders. There was a snap of breaking bones. One dragon carried away the left arm and the banner. The other dragon took the rest. Blood was swirling in the air.

The dragons flew in higher and higher spirals.

At last, the banner dropped from the lifeless arm and fell—a storming red swirl.

Zortan was riding furiously to the north when the falling banner speared him through his left shoulder. He was ripped from his horse, tangled in the banner tongue. Writhing on the ground, heavy gold chains—gaudy, mismatched, and chaotic—tangled, twisted, and knotted—reflected the dragons' fire.

He struggled to stand.

A dragon with blue eyes torched him.

Zortan ran screaming and thrashing, the flaming banner swirling red.

Another dragon torched him, and there was an explosion of putrefying vapors.

The huge dragons with blue eyes circled the burning beastly men, torching them with almost invisible heat.

The fire became white. And then everything was gone. Nothing but ashes—the dust of The Plain.

The dragons flew off to the south. Except three. They were the small type, with keen red eyes. Searching, they circled the ashes. Then, one of them looked toward the watchtower. It broke away from the circle and flew straight toward Artama.

Their eyes met.

Artama did not move, and he did not blink.

The dragon pulled back, hovered, and then flew away, rejoining the others.

The three dragons flew off to the south.

Hours passed. Shadows lengthened.

Artama did not think in words. He envisioned. The gray clouds shifted and took shape as dragons . . . and then gradually swirled away.

The sun began to set.

Artama stood and staggered to the rim of the watchtower. He looked over the edge. In the shadow of the tower, he saw the dying dragon, shimmering with heat, beginning to evaporate.

Artama looked toward the setting sun turning gold.

He lost all sense of time.

His face was crusted with blood, and his forehead was throbbing with pain.

He had no blanket.

He had no water.

He had no food.

But he had the needlebox.

Today was the day it had to be.

And he knew he was free.

In the middle of eternity, in the desolation, Artama watched a spider weaving a web between two rocks. The spider ran splendid spokes and then added concentric polygons . . . miraculous and common . . . spectacular and mundane.

Eventually, it grew dark.

Lying on his back exhausted, Artama studied the stars.

He began to wonder: What are they, *really*? *Where* are they? He began to see dragons in the stars, as he had seen in the clouds.

Artama followed the moon across the sky. He thought about the shape of the dragon on the moon, always there, constant. He thought about The Town, and he thought about his father and The Readers, and he thought about Kora . . . across The Plain.

He felt far away . . . far away from everything.

Gradually, the number of stars became incomprehensible . . . billions upon billions upon trillions . . . .

The silence was profound.

Shooting stars were everywhere.

And then he spotted one specifically.

He thought it stopped . . . hovered . . . and then shot away.

A shiver crossed his shoulders.

Eventually, Artama fell asleep . . . into the blue and gold and white.

4

ARTAMA HEARD VOICES, voices that were pure. The harmony resonated and reverberated . . . . He could not recognize the voices, nor could he understand them. But he understood, nonetheless. He had no sense of time. He felt far away, far away from everything—except the voices. They were near him. They were inside him. He thought his eyes were closed. He knew they were not open. Yet he could see the colors of the chorus, the pure voices, the song everlasting, beyond the blue and gold and white.

In the center of his forehead, Artama felt a soothing touch. He remembered the rock when it hit—heavy and sharp. His blood swirling in the air—bright and red. He remembered the dragon evaporating.

And he remembered the countless stars.

He felt the touch, and he inhaled a fragrance . . . a fragrance he knew . . . but could not name . . . redolent of miraculous healing.

He could feel someone breathing.

It was quiet. Nothing was ever more quiet: the quiet of the moment before The Beginning, before the singularity.

He saw only blue and gold now . . . and a black line curving, tipped with glowing orange.

He realized he was staring at a candle flame.

Artama heard the chorus again, and within the chorus, he heard his name. Now, he recognized a voice—her voice. The fragrance . . . the touch . . . . It was Kora!

His forehead was suddenly radiant. Was it a kiss?

Now, it was quiet again, as quiet as the point of no return, the edge of a black hole, an event horizon.

Artama was lying on a bed, in clothes of the style he was given on his first journey, like those he wore as he stood in The Hall and challenged The Readers, the clothes made of the unknown fabric.

He looked around the room. To the left was a window. Farther to the right, in the corner, was a triangular table. On the table was a brilliant yellow bowl filled with the red fruit of the weebon tree. To the right of the table, leaning against the wall, was a stringed musical instrument unknown to Artama.

He recalled home, The Town. Looking up from his book, the late-afternoon golden sunlight was glowing through the window. The reading table was stacked with books. On one of the stacks, near the window, was a bowl of weebons, and Artama noted a weeworm crawling from one weebon to another.

Next to the bowl on the triangular table, he saw the needlebox.

His spirit soared!

Next, he saw the door.

To the right, beyond the foot of the bed, was another table, a circular table with five chairs. Beyond the table was a bookcase, and perched on the bookcase were exquisitely carved dragons with roaring open mouths and swirling tongues of dragon-fire.

There was a knock on the door. Artama could not think of a word to say, and although he felt weak, he stood.

The door opened, and Kora appeared.

She was no longer a child.

Kora had long dark hair and deep dark eternal eyes. Her body was gracefully curved. She wore golden hoop earrings and a golden pendant—a talisman—a golden coin struck with the image of a dragon.

Artama felt a stirring he had never known before, and he knew he would never be the same.

Resplendently, Kora smiled. "I brought water from the golden fountain." She poured the water from a jar into a cup and handed it to Artama. "I am *so* glad to see you."

In the cup, Artama noted the bubbles. For a moment they appeared, tended to gather and merge, and at last, they burst—becoming one with the air.

Kora repeated, "It is so good to see you—to see you *here*

. . . *alive, real*. I saw what was happening while *Visioning*. I saw Zortan and the beastly men approaching The Town. I saw you in The Hall, and I saw The Game . . . and the dragons."

"Every day I thought of you," Artama said.

Kora blushed. "I know."

There was an awkward, quiet moment.

Artama asked Kora about the bookcase and the exquisitely carved dragons.

"We honor both books and dragons," she answered. "We respect them. The books . . . because they are a *technological* wonder, a magnificent manner of recording thoughts. The dragons . . . because they protect us. They are faultless judges of the heart. They guard the gates— the *portals*. They guard us."

Kora motioned toward the bookcase. "We cherish the books, although they are obsolete—archaic. They are more than technology. They are intrinsically beautiful— each an *objet d'art*."

"What do you mean?"

"It is *French*, a beautiful language—from another world, another earth, another time. It simply means object of art."

"Where do you learn these things: Visioning, French, another world, another earth . . . another time?"

"At *The Academy*."

"What is The Academy?"

"You are *here*. You are where you need to be now. *This* is The Academy."

Thinking, Artama paused. He did not understand Visioning or French or other worlds or portals . . . .

He asked, "Are the dragons mortal?"

"No more than you." And then Kora added, "It is a matter of the heart—as you know—a matter of the spirit, a matter of the soul."

In his mind, Artama saw the bowl of weebons and the weeworm crawling from one weebon to another.

Kora said, "I prayed for you."

Again, Artama was at a loss for words.

"As for the beastly men," Kora continued, "they lived

by fire, and so—by fire—they died. Their hearts were as hard as the blade of a sword, and they died by a sword—the sword of fire."

Kora put her hand on Artama's chest, and for a moment, he was breathless. She said, "It is about what is *here*. Of course, it is not about gold. What good is gold, without water?"

Curiously, Kora looked at Artama and said, "I have always wondered . . . . The first time, when you set out to cross The Plain, what did you hope to find?"

"I wanted to see for myself . . . . I wanted to see for myself if there were dragons. And I hoped to look over the edge."

"What do you mean?"

"I hoped to see if there were *truly* dragons. And, eventually, I hoped to look over the edge of the earth. I hoped to see what supports it."

Kora laughed.

And then she blushed again. "I am *so* sorry, Artama."

Artama blushed too.

Silence.

The moment before the singularity.

Kora spoke first, "But, Artama, the earth is *round*."

"What do you mean?"

"I mean the earth is a *sphere*, like a weebon. There is no edge." Kora walked toward the triangular table.

Artama was fascinated.

Kora picked a weebon from the bowl and held it out toward him. "No edge."

He rephrased, "But what supports the earth?"

"This is discussed in many ways." Kora reflected for a moment. "I would say it is the interplay of forces."

"What do you mean?"

"In a sense, it is floating."

Artama relived walking through the crowd toward the red horizon. Things had never looked so clear. The air was clean. Everything was crystal at the edge. Artama was in the moment . . . in the middle of eternity. He had no sense of fear. He had no sense of time. He was . . . *there*. Floating in the center of infinity. Immortal.

"Floating?" he asked.

"As the result of the interplay of forces." Kora thought more, but there were no words in Artama's language.

Artama said, "If the earth were round, people would fall off."

Kora responded, "*Gravity.*"

"Gravity?"

Kora moved toward Artama and said, "Every particle of matter in the *universe* attracts every other particle." After another moment of thought, she added, "Gravity attracts toward the center of *mass* of the object—but that is for the professors at The Academy to discuss. Your earth attracts you toward its center, whether you are on the top or the bottom . . . or the side. Really, there is no top or bottom or side. It is only a point of view."

He put his hand to his forehead, to his aching wound.

Knowingly, Kora said, "Your wound will heal. You will bear a scar, but it will be a radiant mark of honor. I used the golden ointment."

Artama asked, "If my world is round and floating, and

if the sun does not rise or set over the earth, then how is there day and night?"

Kora walked to the triangular table and picked up the brilliant yellow bowl of weebons.

Artama was lost in admiration.

Kora carried the bowl to the table in front of the bookcase and placed it at the center. She set one weebon near the edge of the table. "The bowl is the sun, *your* sun," she said. "The weebon is the earth, *your* earth. Your earth *rotates*." Kora slowly turned the weebon. "The sun illuminates the portion of the earth turned toward it. One rotation is one day. Your world turns toward the sun, to the east: sunrise. When your point of view turns past the sun, to the west: sunset."

Artama mused:

> *Where the sun rises—as the yeast in bread—*
> *We call East.*
> *Where the sun sets—for a night of rest—*
> *We call West.*

Everything seemed miraculous. Why not one more

thing?

Then, Artama asked again, "But what supports the earth?"

Kora answered, "Gravity . . . *velocity* . . . . The interplay of forces." She paused. "The earth *orbits* the sun."

Artama said, "Tell me about The Academy."

Kora took his hand.

"I told you. You are *here*." She waved her free hand toward the solar system on the table and continued, "The earth is attracted to the sun and would be pulled into it, but it has velocity in another direction, away from the sun, *perpendicular* to a line drawn from the center of the sun to the center of the earth. But, again, this is a matter for the Professors." Nonetheless, to finish the thought, Kora carefully added, "This velocity is perfect. In a *vacuum*, in *space*, there is no *friction*, no resistance. The path of the earth is bent, curved by gravity—never escaping the attraction of the sun, never pulling away. And the surface of the sun always curves away as the earth perpetually falls toward it: *orbiting*.

"If you could throw a rock hard enough, with enough force—the *escape velocity*—it would break free of the gravity of the earth. If you threw it with too little velocity, it would fall. If you threw it perfectly, in a vacuum, it would orbit: perpetually falling."

Artama recalled the high arcs of the glowing coals. He relived the moment the rock hit his forehead, and he visualized his blood swirling red in the air . . . .

"Or, if you could shoot an arrow . . . ."

Artama imagined an arrow orbiting. And he shook with the memory of the flaming arrows of the bowmen falling from the sky.

A glint of light from the strings of the instrument caught his eye.

Kora noted this and stopped speaking. She stood and set her chair away from the table. Kora walked to the instrument and took it. "This is a *meteoron*."

Artama was hopelessly, wonderfully lost.

Kora walked back to the chair, seated herself gracefully, and began to play.

The music resonated and reverberated.

The strings were of meteoron—the most musical of metals—and they radiated, glowing blue and gold and white. The body of the instrument was made of curlywood, with an intricate swirling grain. Curlywood gifts a heavenly sound.

Artama could barely breathe.

Kora began to sing:

> God gave unto the world
>
> The gold coin.
>
> The gold is true gold,
>
> And true gold is love.

Kora's voice was exquisitely, unnervingly beautiful.

> The morning was sunlight.
>
> The meadow was green.
>
> On the road the man.
>
> On the meadow the king.
>
> The one and the other
>
> Found the gold coin.

God gave unto the world

The gold coin.

The gold is true gold,

And true gold is love.

The morning was sunlight.

The meadow was green.

On the road the woman.

On the meadow the queen.

The one and the other

Found the gold coin.

There are many mansions.

There are many rooms.

The man and the woman,

The king and the queen—

Each alone in a room—

Set the gold coin on a table at noon.

Kora stopped.

Silence: again the silence of the event horizon, the point of no return.

Kora stood and motioned toward the chair. "Artama, please. I will teach you."

Artama seated himself, and Kora gave him the meteoron. Then she walked around behind the chair.

With her left hand, Kora took Artama's left hand and placed it on the neck of the instrument. She showed him a chord.

Artama recalled the countless stars. He remembered the touch, and he inhaled the fragrance . . . the fragrance he knew and loved . . . the fragrance of miraculous healing.

With her right hand, Kora took Artama's right thumb and strummed the chord. "This we call E minor."

Artama shuddered.

Into the night, Kora taught Artama to play, and they sang about matters of the heart.

"Tell me about Visioning," Artama said the following afternoon. He wanted to understand how Kora saw things.

"It is like seeing the lightning and knowing the thunder will follow . . . or seeing the bell swing in a far away tower and knowing you will hear it ring. Things are seen because they follow naturally. They are there to be seen." Kora paused and then added, "As you know the way across The Plain."

"I do not know the way."

"You cannot *explain* it, but you *know* it."

Once again, Artama knew he would never be the same.

"We are all treasures of knowledge we cannot explain—or understand," Kora continued. "You are here for a reason."

Artama thought he could live here forever.

But he knew he must return.

"Visioning comes to us," Kora stated, "but it can be developed, and we train to improve at The Academy."

Artama moved toward Kora.

"The Academy is where you can learn—where you are free to learn—where you are free to think." She paused. There was some trepidation in her voice when she added,

"*Your* time has come."

"I hope so."

"Eventually, you may think otherwise. This is preparation for many travails."

Kora took Artama's hand. "Walk with me. You should see the outside and breathe fresh air. Walk with me to my favorite place."

Together they left the cottage and walked along a path of flat stones beneath the azure sky. Along the path, deep-green leaves were the background for brilliant flowers of red and yellow and blue and gold and white. Off to the left, and off to the right, other paths led to other cottages. The aroma was the definition of fragrance.

They came upon a golden fountain.

"This is not the one I remember," Artama said.

"We are blessed with many of them. They provide the *living water*—the water I gave you the first time, and the water I gave you yesterday."

Artama could feel his wound healing . . . .

In time, they walked through a stand of weebon trees and came to Kora's place.

The sun was setting.

Kora's place was a pool of the clearest water, surrounded by a low stone wall. The pool was perpetually filled by a spring: Water flowed over rocks, bubbles appeared and merged and burst . . . and the rocks, gradually . . . over vast time . . . had become rounded stones.

A shiver crossed Artama's shoulders.

In so many ways, things seemed so much the same, the way they were at home, in The Town, in *his* world: the sunset . . . the bubbles on the water . . . the weebon trees.

Yet, here, two moons were visible to the east.

"At home . . ." Artama was struggling for words, "there is only one moon: the dragon moon."

Kora did not immediately respond. Then she said, "When I can, I come here at night and swim alone. I float in the water, and I think about the interplay of forces . . . . I admire the stars from my point of view."

Kora paused and then added wistfully, "I wish you

could stay."

Artama was looking at a weebon tree, studying a weeworm spinning a cocoon. "When can I actually attend The Academy?"

"Tomorrow."

"In less than one rotation." Artama smiled.

Kora smiled too.

Artama wanted everything. He wanted to stay. He wanted to learn. He wanted to know Kora. And he knew, eventually, he must return. He must tell his father—his father must know. And The Readers—and the people— must know.

"I assume, then, my moon orbits my earth, just as my earth orbits my sun," he said. "But why do I always see the dragon—it never changes?"

"Gravity, again. *Synchronization*. Your moon orbits, but over vast time, the force of gravity has locked the rotation and *synchronized* it. You always see the dragon, because your moon rotates slowly. One rotation for each orbit: synchronization."

"Why has the rotation of the earth not locked with the sun?"

Kora winked. "A good question."

"I know . . . ." Artama smiled. "The Academy."

Artama picked two weebons from the weebon tree and held them as though they were his earth and his moon. "If the moon orbits the earth with the dragon always visible, then on the far side, if people were building uncountable signal fires, I would never see them. I would never know they exist. And those living *there*—on the far side of the moon—would never see my world. They would always be looking away. To them, I would not exist."

Kora smiled. "Truly, the unknown is limitless."

5

IN THE GREAT HALL of The Academy of Anagnorisis, in the large antechamber of The Headmaster's office, Artama was seated in a high-backed upholstered chair, waiting in unsettled anticipation. On a window ledge, a cat was sleeping in the golden afternoon sunlight.

Artama considered the room. The golden glowing windows and the sleeping cat were to the left. The windows were tall, and the entire wall was aglow. The cat was the color of the dust of The Plain, and its whiskers were gold. Immediately before Artama was the door to The Headmaster's office—a heavy dark wooden door carved with dragons and swirling fire. To the right were bookcases—heavy dark wooden bookcases filled with ancient volumes, more books than Artama had ever imagined. In front of the bookcases were two circular tables. On one table were three globes, each with a different pattern of blue and green and tan and white, each held in a dark wooden stand carved with the fire of dragons. Above the table on the wall, between two bookcases, hung a mirror in an ornately carved golden frame of swirling dragon-fire.

Artama stood and walked toward the table.

The cat jumped down from the window ledge.

Artama studied the globes.

The cat rubbed against his ankles.

Eventually, Artama raised his eyes to his image in the mirror. In the center of his forehead was a golden glowing star: a sunburst.

He looked to the globes again.

He felt as though he were floating: the interplay of forces.

Artama turned to the mirror again and studied

the glowing sun in the center of his forehead, the consummation of the impact of the rock and the golden ointment and Kora's kiss.

Artama looked to the other table. In the center was a solitary clear orb. He walked to the table and looked more closely. In the center of the orb—suspended—was a tiny rectangular object.

The cat rubbed against his ankles.

The door opened and a tall man in a black official robe beckoned, "Headmaster Thorne welcomes you."

The cat scooted through the doorway first.

Artama followed.

Immediately, he was drawn into the eyes of The Headmaster, and Artama saw his world: The Town, the azure sky, the storming red swirl—blood in the air.

Headmaster Thorne wore a robe of the deepest blue. His smile was kindly. His hair and beard were white and long. Lines around his eyes were like artful grooves in a pattern on pottery.

Artama visualized his father painting storming red

swirls on the pottery that Artama made from the clay from the riverbank on the edge of The Plain.

Artama looked quickly around the room. Again, the walls were bookcases . . . and displays of swords.

He gazed once more into the eyes of The Headmaster, and now he saw things he did not recognize: solar systems and galaxies—all swirling. Artama felt as though he were floating again . . . .

The Headmaster smiled encouragingly. "Kora speaks proudly of you." He paused. "This must be overwhelming."

"Yes, sir."

"Please be seated. Be comfortable."

Artama sat in another high-backed upholstered chair.

The Headmaster poured water from a pitcher into a cup and gave it to Artama.

Artama noted the bubbles, and he struggled to collect his thoughts. "I have many questions."

"I know," Thorne spoke. "We want you to return with knowledge . . . and wisdom. What would you like to know?"

"Everything."

The Headmaster laughed softly.

"To begin with," Artama said, "what are the three spheres?"

"Models. Our world—we often refer to it as E1, another world—called E2, and your world—E3."

"Models?"

"Miniatures. Likenesses."

"You study my world?"

"We study both your world and E2. In all of infinity and eternity, these are the only two worlds with life—life similar to ours—we have ever found.

"We frequently refer to E2. It is a point of reference, a mid-point. The people of E2 have made many great advances, and they have also suffered greatly. Unfortunately, we have seen the infortunate course of E2.

"We study your world because it is younger, and we might be able to help."

The cat jumped onto Artama's lap.

Artama set the cup on a circular table next to the chair

and absently began rubbing under the cat's chin. The cat began to purr.

"Elladora seems to like you." The Headmaster chuckled.

"A beautiful creature."

"And like a dragon, she is a faultless judge of the heart."

"The solitary sphere . . . the clear orb? What is in the center?"

"A chip. A *microchip*. It is a fragment, a remnant, a preserved relic. On E2, for a time, these were embedded in the brains of the people. It proved to be a disaster."

"In so many ways everything seems the same, yet . . . ."

"In so many ways everything *is* the same, *except* . . . all that is different." The Headmaster chuckled again.

Artama's eyes were drawn to a large fishbowl—a truncated globe—on another circular table. Large bewildering fish swam lyrically.

"Few have seen an attack of the dragons and lived to tell about it," stated The Headmaster. He then opened a drawer on the right of his desk and withdrew an object—a simple rectangle, perfectly clear—the size of a small book. He placed it on top of his desk. "We call it a *crystal*, although technically, it is not. Nonetheless . . . a device you will find extremely helpful." Thorne gave the crystal to Artama. "Professor Halpinson will instruct you in its use."

The surface of the crystal was firmly soft like flesh over bone.

"Enjoy your time here, Artama. You will long for these days," The Headmaster spoke solemnly. He nodded toward the man in the black official robe, "Bradle will guide you through the corridors and show you to your chamber. Bradle speaks your language, as does Professor Halpinson. In the general population, it is not common, but here at Anagnorisis, it is not unusual."

Artama gently lifted Elladora from his lap and set her on the stone floor. Then he stood.

The Headmaster spoke, "The Law of Gravity contains the answer. As does time, of course."

"Sir?"

"You were curious as to why your earth has not synchronized with your sun."

"Oh."

"Zana's Law of Gravity. Every particle of matter in the universe attracts every other particle. On E2 it is known as Newton's Law of Gravity. On your planet, no one has recognized it yet."

Artama chuckled.

The Headmaster continued, "The force of the attraction is proportional to the product of the two masses and inversely proportional to the square of the distance between them. The larger the object, the greater the attraction. But as the distance between the objects increases, the force of the attraction dramatically decreases.

"E2, for example, has not yet synchronized with its sun either. Although the mass of the sun is unthinkably greater than the mass of the earth, the distance between them is also unthinkable. The attraction of the sun is greatly lessened by the unimaginable distance. So it is with your world. Nonetheless, given enough time, your earth would synchronize with your sun. Except for the moon. The earth would synchronize with the moon first. Although the moon is much smaller than the sun, it is much closer and has a greater gravitational force. Likewise for E2. But the dying suns will destroy everything first."

Artama looked grave.

"Do not worry. It will take an unimaginably long time." The Headmaster smiled and waved his hand.

"I have many questions."

Thorne nodded understandingly and concluded, "Bradle will take you to your study chamber straightaway, and you can begin learning to use the crystal. You will get your answers."

The Headmaster stood and extended his hand.

Artama reached out, and they shook hands— cosmically.

"Thank you, sir."

The Headmaster smiled. "You are welcome, Artama. Until our next meeting."

Bradle walked along a long corridor. The walls were

paneled in radiant dark wood. Bradle's strides were quick. Artama walked apace. The corridor was glowing in golden light, in the light of incandescent orbs. On each side of the corridor were doors—choices. Bradle stopped at a door on the right. He took a probe from his robe and slid it into the lock. They entered the study chamber.

At the front of the room were a small rectangular table and a solitary chair.

"This is your study chamber," said Bradle as they walked to the table. "Here you may practice in peace." Bradle gave Artama the key.

Artama withdrew the crystal from his pocket, thinking about the needlebox.

"Place it on the table," Bradle said, "and place two fingers on it, your first and second. Now think, Artama. Thoughts precede. What would you like to know?"

On the tips of his fingers Artama felt the crystal warming.

"Simply say, 'On,'" Bradle instructed.

"On."

The crystal began to glow.

"After awhile you will not need to speak—the crystal will read your mind."

Artama withdrew his hand and considered the situation . . . for better or for worse.

"And now, may I introduce Professor Halpinson?" Bradle continued.

A ray of light shot straight up from the crystal. An electric humming passed through Artama's mind. The ray of light began to open—like a peacock tail—and then swirled in upon itself and became a man in a black academic robe.

"Hello, Artama. It is good to meet you at last."

Artama was speechless.

"I will be instructing you, guiding you," stated Professor Halpinson.

Bradle nodded to Artama and turned . . . . He was at the door. "It was an honor meeting you," he said. The door opened and closed, and he was gone.

Professor Halpinson asked, "You have questions?"

Artama was taken by a vision of his father. And he saw the people building a wall around The Town.

"What are you?" Artama asked and reached out to touch it.

"I am a halpin. Like a hologram."

"I do not understand."

"I know, but in time you will." Professor Halpinson held his arms out and turned around in a complete circle. At first slowly, and then faster and faster until, abruptly, he stopped. "I was . . . we were developed by the Halpin Team. I am, like the others, a son of Halpin."

Professor Halpinson moved aside and showed Artama how to bring up a screen. The screen—a translucent phenomenon that showed everything clearly—displayed text and images. And the text and images accelerated, driving information into Artama's mind. And there was sound. Sound reminiscent of the voices that were pure. The harmony resonated and reverberated inside his mind. He thought his eyes were closed . . . . He could see the colors of the chorus, the pure voices, the song everlasting beyond the blue and gold and white.

"The crystal is at your command now. Talk to it. To start, just ask questions. Within its limits it will amaze you. Shortly, it will understand you, and you will not need to speak—just think."

A halpin of Kora briefly appeared.

Professor Halpinson chuckled. "As I said."

The screen pulsed and drew Artama's attention.

Zana's Law—in text and images and sound—was driven into his mind.

Artama studied, practiced, and learned . . . and lost all sense of time.

In The Library Archives, the students were illuminated in the blue light of their screens and halpins. The Archives held thousands and thousands and thousands of books on shelves of dark wooden bookcases, in the light of glowing golden orbs. Among the bookcases were sculptures and paintings.

As amazing as the crystal was, Artama cherished the

books. He selected a volume and took it to a table. He inhaled the fragrance and thought of his home, his father, the cottage, and the stacks of books on the reading table. He recalled the vision of the people of The Town building the wall. He needed to return, and he longed to stay.

Artama was now faced with a decision.

Thousands and thousands and thousands of books.

Billions and billions and trillions of stars.

A googol and a googol again.

Unto a googolplexian.

One choice to make.

Artama studied diligently. He studied Del't, the language of The Academy. He studied mathematics, physics, chemistry, biology, medicine, astronomy, navigation, cartography, philosophy, religion, meditation, astrology, literature, music, painting, sculpture, metallurgy, economics, politics, military strategy, martial arts, swordsmanship . . . and Visioning. He studied comparative studies, and he studied the study of studies.

Swordsmanship enticed him: He wanted to be able to defeat brutish ignorance on its own terms. He would never forget the guards and his humiliation. He saw his blood swirling in the air.

In The Oron Center, Artama trained with Antag, The Academy Master of Swordsmanship. The Center was a massive facility with many levels. The Swordsmanship Level was a stage upon which fierce training battles were fought. Many lessons were learned, many questions answered.

Antag was tall and dark, with broad shoulders and strong arms. His gray hair was short. A scar crossed his nose horizontally and continued under his left eye. His tunic was crimson.

He raised his sword above his head and began turning . . . at first slowly . . . and then faster and faster until he became a mesmerizing storming red swirl . . . .

And then, abruptly, he stopped.

"As I have said, we practice the sword as a discipline, for the sake of discipline. Focus. Concentration. To keep strong and alert. But *you—Artama—*will need these skills in fights for your life."

Without warning, Antag attacked.

Clang!

"In your life, the time is coming, as surely as the sunrise, when you will no longer be able to win by your cleverness alone."

Clang!

"You will need physical strength and stamina."

Clang!

"You will need heart. Not just the goodness you have shown . . . but the heart of a warrior."

Clang!

Sparks flew—blue and gold and white.

Again, Antag began to spin into a storming red swirl.

Likewise, Artama spun.

Suddenly, they stopped, facing one another.

"Attack!" shouted Antag.

Artama lunged into battle, and Antag took Artama off his feet with a sweep of his legs.

Artama was on his back on the ground, with the tip of Antag's sword at his throat.

Visioning troubled Artama: He could see sounds and hear sights. He saw his father growing despondent. He saw the people of The Town building a fortress, encircling their homes. In his vision, the people looked like halpins, as translucent as the base of a candle flame. Artama wondered about reality. And then he laughed.

To reassure himself, he poured water from a pitcher into a cup. He noted the bubbles on the water in the cup. For a moment they appeared, tended to gather and merge, and at last, they burst—becoming one with the air.

The bubbles evoked the memory of the weeworm crawling from one weebon to another—in the bowl, on the stack of books, on the table, near the window, in the workshop . . . in the cottage . . . in The Town . . . near The Plain . . . in the land where—once—the people were almost always content.

Artama remembered the loud knock on the door and

the urgent cry of Taladar.

He knew he must return. He must comfort his father . . . and enlighten the people. But he longed to stay with Kora.

Once again, in The Great Hall of The Academy, in the large antechamber of The Headmaster's office, Artama was seated in the high-backed upholstered chair, waiting in determined anticipation. On the window ledge, Elladora was sleeping in the glowing golden afternoon sunlight. Artama felt cold, very cold. He felt his blood moving from his arms and legs to warm his core. His hands were frigid. His mouth was dry. A shiver crossed his shoulders.

Immediately before Artama was the door to The Headmaster's office—the heavy dark wooden door carved with dragons and swirling fire. And now, it was also the door to his father, The Town . . . and the storming red swirl.

Artama looked at the bookcases, tables, and globes. And the mirror. He walked to the globes and pondered.

The golden afternoon sunlight burnished everything.

The door opened.

Bradle was standing in the doorway smiling. "The Headmaster welcomes you."

Artama walked eagerly through the doorway.

Elladora followed.

The Headmaster motioned, and Artama took the high-backed upholstered chair.

Thorne poured water for Artama and gave him the cup. "Good afternoon. What is on your mind?"

Elladora jumped onto Artama's lap. Immediately, her warmth infused him.

Artama's mouth was still dry. He took a sip from the cup and then set it on the table. "I want to return. I want to return to The Town . . . my people . . . and help."

Silence.

"And I want to stay with Kora."

Bradle excused himself, adding, "It is an honor knowing you." He exited through the door to the corridors.

"Of course we knew this time would come." Thorne

smiled. "It is your destiny."

"It is breaking my heart," Artama confessed.

"You will find your world brutish. Some will think you are an angel . . . even a god. Some will think you are a demon . . . even a devil. But, of course, things are not always as they seem."

Artama placed Elladora on the floor, and then he stood and walked to the fishbowl. He reached in and withdrew two fish in his cupped hand. Out of the bowl, held in his hand, the fish were small. "Things are not always as they seem." Artama put the fish back in the bowl. Large again.

The Headmaster chuckled appreciatively. Then he said, "Now, I ask you for your crystal."

"But . . . ."

"It would be useless, Artama. The energy required is unthinkable on E3. But to replace it, I give you this." Thorne stood and walked to the first display of swords and reached for a simple hilt. He whirled the sword above his head and then pointed it toward the floor. There was no visible blade. Yet, the air was distorted as the blade passed through it, like the shimmering air in the heat of The Plain. Thorne walked toward Artama. "This magnificent invisible blade will be much more useful. I give you *The Crystal*."

Artama shivered. He was floating in the middle of infinity . . . in the center of eternity. Solemnly he asked, "What is breaking my heart?"

"Love."

6

ARTAMA KNEW he was seeing everything for the last time. Tonight was his final night on E1, his last night with Kora.

The preparations for his return were finished.

Artama was walking toward Kora's place. The afternoon sky was splendidly bright, painfully bright, but there was no time to enjoy the beauty, even though he tried to memorize it, for Artama was caught in the rush of events.

The afternoon sky reminded Artama of the first morning sky of Zortan's march and the endless vastness of The Plain. Zortan invaded Artama's thoughts. He relived

The Game and the old man screaming as he was buried in glowing coals. Artama considered everything he was leaving. He knew he was leaving intelligent peace and returning to ignorant war.

The Headmaster had taken the crystal and given him the sword with the magnificent invisible blade—The Crystal.

More than once in conversation, Thorne had warned Artama, "When you return, your mind will become clouded. Although, you will have lucid moments."

The moons were beginning to rise above the eastern horizon.

Approaching the golden fountain, the colors were brilliant red and yellow and blue and gold and white, against the deepest green. Artama inhaled the aroma. He stopped and watched the water cascading down the fountain. He remembered the first time he saw Kora: He was looking out the window. She was at the fountain. It felt like a dream. And now, when he returned to The Town, how could he explain everything? Artama cupped his hands and scooped water from the fountain. He drank. A shiver shook his body. Artama took a last look around. He remembered walking from The Town toward Zortan, and Artama started walking toward Kora's place again.

Anon, Artama arrived and made his way through the entrance of the grove of weebon trees. Now, before him was the pool, Kora's pool, the clear water. Surrounding the pool was the low stone wall. He walked to it and sat. He pondered the glint of sunlight on the water. What was he doing? What was he thinking? He was leaving paradise. Leaving Kora. But he must. To help his father and the people of The Town.

The trees were covered in silky white weeworm cocoons. One in particular caught Artama's attention. As it shuddered, Artama shuddered too. He could be killed by people who did not understand. A warm breeze moved among the weebon trees, and the cocoon twitched again.

And then he heard Kora stepping through the entrance. How much time had passed?

Kora carried a small pack and a meteoron case. In the

darkening golden light, Kora smiled for Artama. She set the pack on top of the stone wall and leaned the meteoron case against it.

Kora walked to Artama and took his hands. She smiled wanly and said, "We always knew this time would come. We always knew you would return."

The clouds were turning purple.

"You know I want to stay."

"And I know you must return."

Artama and Kora embraced.

In time, Kora stepped back, took Artama by the hand and guided him to the pack and the meteoron case. They sat on the wall.

"The Headmaster has attended to your survival. You will have water and food and a blanket and a lighter. And a map, of course. And The Crystal." Kora's smile brightened, and she added, "I have packed a few other things for you."

Kora opened the pack and removed a neatly folded scarf. Unfolding it revealed a block of chocolate. She broke off a chunk, took a small bite, and gave the rest to Artama.

Transcending bittersweetness.

Kora removed a nutshell containing the amber ointment, the ointment that brought sight to his father. "The nutshell is a token of the first time."

Then, she removed a small jar. She opened it, and the jar emitted a golden glow. "The golden ointment, of course."

Next, Kora removed a candle. "Because a candle flame is a constant in our worlds."

And finally, she removed the needlebox. "Still useful."

Kora began repacking. "There are a couple of surprises at the bottom." She smiled mischievously. "Some of these things you will need, others you will simply be glad you have, one will be lost along the way." She winked and closed the pack.

Kora turned toward the meteoron case. It was midnight blue, soft but resilient. She unzipped the case and removed the instrument. Kora began to play, and the strings began to glimmer in blue and gold and white.

Artama noted other cocoons beginning to shudder

and wiggle. He stood and walked to a weebon tree and watched intently as one cocoon began to split, emitting a gentle golden glow.

The gold of the sun was deepening, and the purple clouds stretched across the sky.

Kora began to sing:

> I came for you.
>
> I came for anyone in pain,
>
> And you know I return,
>
> And you know I remain.
>
> Do you remember?
>
> A few people do.
>
> As old as the hills . . .
>
> Older than Evil . . .
>
> One Love . . . .
>
> I came for you.
>
> I came for anyone in pain,
>
> And you know I return,

And you know I remain.

I remember uneven ground . . .

Men looking for gold,

Looking for power,

Looking in vain.

And fallen on the uneven ground

Were men without gold,

Without power,

Burning,

Crying in vain.

I came for you.

I came for anyone in pain,

And you know I return,

And you know I remain . . .

One Love.

Artama thought about his father painting the storming red swirl, the bubbles in the cup, and the weeworm crawling from one weebon to another—in the bowl, on the stack of books, on the table, near the window, in the workshop . . . in the cottage . . . in The Town . . . near The Plain . . . in the land where—once—the people were almost always content.

Another cocoon began to split, another golden glow.

Artama turned and walked back to Kora. She passed him the meteoron.

Artama sat on the stone wall and began to play.

Tears came to Kora's eyes.

Artama played beautifully, and he sang:

> I remember,
>
> Before I came,
>
> Before my name and number.
>
> I remember, and I dream.
>
>
> Like a memory,
>
> I wander around
>
> Looking for you—
>
> Finding my way home.

Beyond the blue and gold and white,

From the moment before

The perfect crystal sunlight

Began shining—

Seemingly, for evermore . . . .

Like a memory,

I wander around

Looking for you—

Finding my way home.

I remember,

Before I came,

Before my name and number.

I remember, and I dream.

Other cocoons began to open incandescently.

The purple clouds grew darker.

Artama leaned the meteoron against the wall.

Kora rose and then kneeled before Artama. She lifted

her gold chain over her head and settled it around Artama's

neck. The talisman—the gold coin struck with the dragon of the dragon moon—rested on Artama's chest. It held the warmth of Kora. "This will serve you well. Remember me. Dream of me. Include me in your prayers. I will pray for you."

"I will."

"Be careful what you reveal," she advised.

Kora stood and stepped back. She sat on the wall.

Artama was enchanted by the glowing of the opening cocoons. He stood and walked back to the trees to get a closer look. He focused on one chrysalis and the golden light emanating. It shook. It lurched. It twitched. It wiggled and wriggled.

In time, Artama turned, but he did not see Kora.

He saw her dress laid over the stone wall.

Then, her head emerged from the water.

She laughed and called, "Come in!" and dived below the surface again.

Artama knew, once more, he would never be the same. He looked back to the opening cocoons, the swell of incandescence. He looked back toward the pool.

Kora's face reappeared.

"Come on!" she shouted. "We can watch the sunset." Kora turned away, looking toward the fading golden light. Floating on her back, she tilted her head back into the water and gazed into the purple and gold.

Artama undressed.

He stepped onto the wall, facing the pool. The talisman glowed softly. He stood for a moment, took a deep breath, and then he dived into the water. The pool was delightfully comfortable, neither cool nor warm: perfect.

Kora rolled over and dived again.

Under the water, their eyes met in deep vision. Everything was flowing crystal at the edge. And now, Artama had time to enjoy it. He was safe . . . in the moment . . . in the middle of eternity. There was no time. He was *there*. Floating in the center of infinity. Immortal.

Lost in Kora's eyes, Artama saw his earth orbiting his sun, and he saw the dragon moon orbiting his earth. Artama saw clearly . . . eternally . . . infinitely . . . now.

Another split cocoon trembled, and ever so slowly, a glorious golden butterfly emerged.

One by one, the cocoons opened, and as night fell, the weebon trees glowed in the aura of the metamorphoses. The golden butterflies lifted, swimming erratically into the night.

7

THERE WAS A FLASH of blue and gold and white.

When he awoke, it felt like a dream.

Lying on his back, Artama felt light, buoyant, translucent, ethereal. He realized he was on the watchtower, looking into the sky. The sky was clear blue, just as he remembered—now with white cumulus clouds. He organized faces: his father, The Readers, Thorne, Kora.

He shivered in the afternoon heat.

The sun, beginning to set, was becoming golden.

Eventually, Artama began to feel heavier and more solid. He rolled onto his side. He saw two packs, the meteoron case, a blanket, and The Crystal in its scabbard.

He looked to the rocks that formed the wall around the rim of the watchtower. In the golden light, he saw a dusty golden spider. In the silence, Artama watched the spider weave a web between two rocks. The spider ran splendid spokes and then added concentric polygons . . . miraculous and common . . . spectacular and mundane.

How much time had passed?

Artama stood and walked slowly, awkwardly, to the rim, and he leaned forward onto the rocks of the wall and looked out over the dust of The Plain. Clean and smooth, still shimmering with heat. There was no sign of conflict. There was no sign of evil. To the east, the sky was tending toward indigo.

Artama turned and looked to the packs and the case. He walked back to them, a little more steadily. He opened Thorne's pack. On top were a map and a telescope. Artama chuckled. See where you are going, and see it from afar. Underneath, a canteen of water and small packets of food. At the bottom, a lighter.

Artama unfolded the map. A circle was drawn around

an area marked "Two Towers."

He opened Kora's pack. Chocolate and the needlebox. Bittersweet direction. He found the nutshell filled with amber ointment, the small jar filled with golden ointment, and the candle. At the bottom, a gold coin. And a picture of Kora. The coin was struck on one side with an image of two moons. On the other side, a sun. The picture was of Kora standing by a fountain of living water, holding a jar.

Artama put the coin and the picture in his shirt pocket.

He set the needlebox on a flat stone and watched the needle gently swing. In time, the needle settled. With the telescope, Artama scanned the horizon for markers, and he saw the Two Towers. They would be his guides. Tomorrow, he could walk to them by afternoon.

Artama was feeling strangely heavy and tired. He knew he should rest, he should sleep. It would be cold tonight, and there was nothing on the watchtower to burn. He knew he did not have the strength to safely work his way down the tower. And even if he found any wood, how could he possibly bring it back to the top? The best thing to do was to stay on the tower. He would be cold, but he would be safe.

He took the canteen from Thorne's pack and hooked it onto his belt. He put the map and the telescope back on top and closed it. Except for the coin and the picture, everything remaining went into Kora's pack. He moved all of the gear to the rocks at the rim.

Artama wrapped himself in the blanket and settled against the wall, for protection—and to benefit from the radiating heat.

In his mind, Artama dived into the perfectly comfortable water of the pool. Under the water, he was lost again in Kora's eyes. He saw his earth orbiting his sun, and he saw the dragon moon orbiting his earth. Everything was flowing crystal at the edge.

That night, when Artama awoke, he beheld the full dragon moon, and he felt terribly alone. He felt far away . . . far away from everything. Lying on his back, he watched the dragon move slowly across the sky. He studied the stars and began to wonder. He thought about his father, The Readers, and The Town . . . and he thought about Kora.

Artama remembered his first journey across The Plain. He wanted to see for himself. Dragons? What was over the edge?

His blind father had encouraged him, blessed him.

Artama remembered seeing Kora for the first time, as she filled the jar with water from the fountain, and he remembered talking with her into the night. She gave him the amber ointment for his father's eyes, and Artama remembered his first jubilant return. He had no fears or doubts. Now, he had both. He had left Kora . . . and the wonder of E1. And now, he had reason to fear men he did not know, for reasons they could not understand. What did the future hold?

Visioning was limited, and he knew it would become more difficult the longer he was on this side.

The stars became incomprehensible in number—billions upon billions upon trillions . . . . The silence was profound. Shooting stars were everywhere. Artama spotted one, specifically . . . .

A shiver crossed his shoulders.

He was not alone.

When Artama awoke on the morning of the second day, he felt rested and more comfortable with his body.

It was time to proceed.

It was another bright day.

Artama rolled the blanket and secured it to the meteoron case with cords. He put the scabbard on his back and adjusted the strap across his chest. Next, he put the packs and the case on his back. He took a few clumsy steps. This was not going to be easy. He walked around the rim of the watchtower, looking for the beginning of his descent. At last, he chose a route.

Artama climbed over the wall and began to work his way down the side. Only five steps down, his right foot slipped on a ledge and sent rocks tumbling and bouncing off the face of the tower, until they hit the ground far below. Artama felt a rush of adrenaline, and he held tight with his hands while blindly searching for another foothold. Shortly, he found one and held steady, trying to stabilize, waiting for his breathing to return to normal. This was real. He was alone, clinging to the face of a rock wall. If he slipped, it would be over. There would be no reunion with his father. There would be no helping the people of The Town. He would never see Kora again. It would all be for nothing.

Carefully, Artama continued, cautiously testing each foothold and handhold, until he reached the ground.

He sat on the rocks around the base of the watchtower and gathered his composure. He removed the picture of Kora from his pocket, looked at it—admiring her dark eyes—and he smiled.

Artama took a deep breath, stood, and started walking toward the Two Towers.

The sun rose higher, and the heat increased.

It was not long before the heat became a burden.

Artama turned to look at the sun. It seemed unusually bright. Gradually, color was bleached from the landscape, and the dust and the rocks and the spires faded into white. As he walked, Artama looked toward the ground. Only periodically would he look to the Towers to confirm his course. In time, the sun was directly overhead, and it was hard to look at anything. Waves of heat shimmered in the distance. The dust of The Plain was blindingly bright. He squinted toward the Two Towers. Something was unusual. The tower on the right was dark. Artama stopped and forced himself to study it. The tower on the right was black.

Artama removed the canteen from his belt and drank. Not much, just enough to wet his mouth and clean his throat. Unless he encountered unexpected adversity, he would have enough water, but unexpected adversity was to be expected. He hooked the canteen back on his belt and started walking toward the Towers.

In a reverie, Artama recalled his home. Comfortable at the reading table. He poured water from the pitcher into the cup and noted the bubbles. For a moment they appeared, tended to gather and merge, and at last, they burst—becoming one with the air.

Eventually, he reached the Two Towers. The one on the left was a spire of white. The one on the right was indeed an oddity, an aberration: a spire of black.

Artama walked to the shaded side of the white tower and removed his burdens, except for the scabbard. He sat and leaned back against the white rocks and looked at the black spire. He drank a little more water. In time, he removed the map, the telescope, and the needle box from the packs. He set the needlebox on the ground and watched the needle settle, pointing toward an empty horizon. He looked through the telescope, but saw only desolation. There were no landmarks. The map would be useless. He would need to use the needlebox as his guide.

Fortunately, there were old dried branches scattered in the dust around the Two Towers. He could, at least, make a small fire. This was undoubtedly the best place to camp for the night. Artama started gathering the meager branches, bringing them back into the shadow of the white spire.

The light began to fade.

Artama heard something. At first, he thought it was the sound of dragons. He stepped out of the shadow and looked to the sky.

Far off, on the western horizon, there was a mountainous wall of dust storming toward him. Artama gathered the map and the telescope and the needlebox and repacked them. He gathered the packs and the case and pushed them into a recess in the base of the white spire. He gathered a few branches and piled them on top, but soon ran out of time. He lay face down on the pile and covered his head with his arms.

The storm hit with horrendous power. Wind blew everywhere. Artama could only wait as the wind howled. Time slowly passed. Artama felt lost, not lost on The Plain, but *lost* . . . alone. Why had he come back?

His last night with Kora came to mind. *"Come on!"* she shouted. *"We can watch the sunset."* Then she turned away, looking toward the fading golden light. Floating on her back, she tilted her head back into the water and gazed into the purple and gold.

The direction of the wind was shifting, slowly coming more at Artama, and eventually, coming from the opposite direction, pummeling him with biting dust. Realizing he had to move to some new shelter, he slid off the branches, onto the ground. He slightly opened his eyes and could see the scant firewood being whipped away in the wind. He closed his eyes and felt for the packs and the case. When he had gathered them all to him, he put his left arm through the straps of the packs and then took the case in both hands. On his stomach, with the case on the ground in front of him, Artama began crawling toward the black spire. The screeching blowing dust was burning his hands. Artama crawled desperately. In time, he came to the protection of the black spire, but the screeching of the wind went on and on and on. His heart was pounding. He felt he was suffocating—bound in a shroud in a grave. He needed to break free and run, but he could not even open his eyes. Everything was black. Forsaken. Into the void, he screamed—a long scream—but all he could hear was the wind.

Silence.

Looking about, Artama slowly stood. Drifts were swirled around the spires. Artama's eyes were burning with dust, and his lips and mouth and throat were dry. He took the canteen from his belt, poured some water into his cupped hand and rinsed his eyes. He took a long drink.

The few branches he had gathered were gone. Soon it would be dark, and it would be another cold night. He shook the dust off of his belongings. He unrolled the blanket and wrapped it around his shoulders. For a while he stared at the fading sunset. Remembering Kora's picture, he retrieved it from his pocket. He looked at it and sighed. How long had he been gone? Two days? He placed Kora's picture on a small drift of dust, took the meteoron from its case, sat on some rocks, and slowly began to play. The music helped. Kora's picture helped.

The music of the meteoron radiated into the cooling air. Artama looked into Kora's eyes, and her eyes held him.

For a moment, he felt well. He could do this. He was not alone. Artama laughed.

In time, night came.

Artama returned the instrument to its case. He sat with the blanket wrapped around him, leaning against the black spire, looking at Kora in the faint light of the rising moon and early stars, and eventually, he fell asleep.

In the morning, Artama awoke cold, stiff, and hungry. He removed a packet of food from Thorne's pack and took a few bites of a thick dark cracker. He drank some water.

He remembered dreaming in the night. In his dream, he was playing the meteoron when the wind came again, blowing dust in his eyes . . . and blowing away the picture of Kora. He put down the instrument and ran after the picture, but it was blowing farther and farther away from him. He ran and ran, futilely, his eyes burning with dust, until he could not see, until he could run no more, and he dropped into the dust. Kora was gone.

Now, in the morning light, Artama walked in an

outward spiral from the Towers, methodically searching, but there was only dust. The picture was gone.

Despondent, Artama walked back to his packs. He removed the needlebox and took a reading. He repacked everything, loaded his burdens on his back, and started walking again.

During the third night, Artama dreamed Kora was singing to him:

You fell—
And felt forsaken—
On the white stone,
Where the wind blew everywhere.
Dust filled the air.
The light began to fade,
But you are not alone.

You fell—
And felt forsaken—
On the black stone,

Where the wind blew everywhere.

Overcome by despair,

As though morning were delayed,

But you are not alone.

A perfect half, I held you,

Until you could laugh,

Where the wind blew everywhere.

You are not alone.

We are not alone.

Artama was walking with his head down. He looked up, occasionally, to check his bearings. There was not much to guide him.

Artama was lost in thought, wondering what he would say when he reached The Town, when suddenly, he shuddered with a presentiment. He looked up, squinting, and scanned the horizon. Almost immediately, he saw two figures, two riders.

To Artama's left, there were some rocks, remnants of a

toppled spire, and he tried to take cover among them.

One of the riders pointed toward Artama, and the two horsemen altered their course and began loping in his direction.

Resigned, Artama stepped forward and continued walking toward the horizon. He was returning to bring good news, a message of hope, but he knew there was trouble ahead.

The two riders drew closer, dust lifting behind them and slowly drifting away.

Artama was eager to talk with someone, but he knew these men were not interested in conversation. He had no choice. He stopped and waved to them. He slipped off his burdens, leaving only the scabbard on his back. He was ready.

At last, near Artama, the riders drew rein, and the horses stopped. The men were dirty and menacing. They reminded Artama of Zortan's men.

Artama shouted, "Hello!"

The riders moved their horses closer. After a moment,

one man spoke. His tone was surly. "What's in the packs?"

"Supplies. Things I need."

The man replied gruffly, "Maybe we need those things more than you."

"I am heading toward The Town. Have you been there recently?"

The other man moved his horse closer, intimidatingly. "What's in that case?"

Artama knew any courtesy could cost him dearly.

The rider said again, "What's in that case?" He drew his sword.

"Nothing of yours."

The other rider drew his sword and snarled, "I'll be the judge of that."

Artama sighed. He drew The Crystal from the scabbard on his back.

The men saw only a hilt, not even a dagger, and they laughed.

The horses began to whinny and shy. The riders spurred them forward, but the horses rose on their hind legs. The men angrily spurred the animals, but they would not advance, and they began to buck.

The riders retreated a few feet, and the horses calmed.

The first man angrily kicked his horse again and shouted. The horse moved forward, but only a length, and then tried to bolt. The rider fought to control the animal, but only after retreating did the horse settle.

The two men looked into each other's eyes.

They dismounted, brandishing their swords.

They began to circle around Artama, and Artama turned with them.

The interplay of forces. Orbiting.

One bandit was trying to work his way around behind Artama, but Artama kept one man on his left and one on his right.

They stopped. Artama could hear them breathing. A horse whinnied.

The bandits attacked, slashing viciously.

Artama spun, parrying, warding off their assault.

There was a fury of rapid cracking sounds and a flurry

of bright flashes.

The horses ran.

The attackers were quickly disarmed, their swords knocked away into the dust.

But not before Artama was wounded.

The bandits fell back, stumbling and tripping. They fell to the ground, scrambling. When they were beyond Artama's sweep, they stopped and looked each other in the eye. They looked at Artama. Awkwardly, both men stood and gradually backed away. Abandoning their swords, they retreated to where the horses had stopped. They mounted and rode away cursing.

Artama examined the wound on the outside of his left shoulder. Fortunately, the blade that struck him was not sharp. Although he was cut, the wound was more like the damage of a club. His shirt had been torn. He ripped off the sleeve, folded it, and held it against the wound, as a dressing. In a short time, the bleeding stopped. That was all he would concern himself with now. He wanted to find a place to camp with some shelter, and tonight, he wanted to have a fire. He hoped there was a suitable campsite over the horizon, some place he could find before nightfall. He gathered his belongings, shouldered them, and wearily started walking.

Pain changes everything. Artama's shoulder was aching badly. The area around the cut was swollen. The wound was now the focus of his attention. Any thoughts of helping his father and the people of The Town were far away on E1.

Artama had found his campsite among a cluster of spires. There were enough dried branches for a small fire, and he was able to sit close to the flames and absorb the warmth. In the firelight, he carefully opened the small jar Kora had packed. The golden glow was reassuring. With his fingertip, he applied a dab of the ointment to the cut and gently smoothed it over the wound. He closed his eyes and felt the healing radiate. He heard the voices, the pure voices, the chorus. The harmony resonated and reverberated. He floated far away from the pain. He could see the colors of the chorus and the song everlasting—the blue and gold and white.

Artama had been walking all day, and he was tired. And he was troubled. He was finding it harder to concentrate. His ability to Vision was weakening. Thorne and Kora had warned him. Several times, he had tried to see his father or Kora, with only tenuous results. He could remember, but Visioning was unclear. He knew he was not alone, but nonetheless, loneliness was emptying him.

In time, as he walked toward the west, toward the reddening sky, something changed with the changing light. He had a sense of something . . . . The Plain was starting to look familiar. He realized he was recognizing spires and rocks. The loneliness began to fade. Hope began to fill him.

Artama stopped. He reached back into Thorne's pack and slid out the telescope. He took a deep breath. He put the telescope to his eye and scanned the horizon. There it was! The Town! Not as he had left it, but as he had

Visioned it. He could see the wall and towers.

Artama hurried onward. He could make it by nightfall! He could be home tonight!

Eventually, Artama stopped to rest, to catch his breath.

The sky to the west was now blood red. He put the telescope to his eye and studied the silhouette of the *fortress*. How different it was. In fact, The Town itself could not be seen at all. A high wall—five times the height of a man—completely blocked any buildings from view. Along the top of the wall were battlements. Artama could see the gate, with a tower on each side, and he could see a guard on each of the towers. Now and then, along the parapet, he could see a guard walking past a crenel. The guards wore uniforms, something Artama had never seen before in his world. Artama had learned about uniforms. These were red, loose, with hoods. What did this mean?

Artama decided to wait until morning.

Huddled by a cluster of rocks, Artama sat in the dark with his blanket wrapped around his shoulders. It was cold, but he did not build a fire. He did not want to reveal himself. He wanted to make his approach in the light of day.

He studied the stars, and he pondered the lonely dragon moon, as white as the robe of The First Reader. He thought about how he used to view the moon—it seemed long ago—before he knew the dragon is merely a phenomenon of sunlight reflecting from the highlands and lowlands of the lunar surface. Now, he knew the mind tended to organize those light and dark areas into that familiar shape, the shape that had been suggested by the elders from the time he was a child.

Artama thought about how he had become accustomed to the moons of E1. They were smaller . . . and appeared smooth, a sandy white. There were no highlands or lowlands or craters, now that he thought about it. For the first time, he wondered: Were they natural, or were they technology?

Where had he gone? Really? Was there a *really*? How long had he been gone?

He remembered the first time he talked with his father

about crossing The Plain. His father had said, *"I am old, and if I travel afar, it will be in your heart. I am blind, and if I see the far edge of The Plain, it will be through your eyes."*

Tomorrow, what would Artama say? He was returning to help, to bring knowledge and wisdom, and hope and comfort . . . . But how could he explain?

Artama touched the talisman on the chain around his neck and closed his eyes. He saw a cocoon tremble and split. Ever so slowly, a glorious golden butterfly emerged.

In the morning, Artama approached The Town.

Today was the day it had to be.

Against the lingering darkness in the west, the light of the rising sun was bright on the wall. The wall was radiant, the color of the dust of The Plain. The gate, made of wood and iron, was as tall as three men. Above the gate were merlons and crenels. On each gate tower, Artama could see a guard in a red uniform.

"Halt!" one guard shouted.

Artama halted.

"Who are you?" the guard yelled. "What is your business?"

"I am Artama. I have come home."

The guard laughed and scoffed, "Artama is dead!"

"I have been away, across The Plain, but I am not dead."

A second guard shouted, "Come closer!"

Artama walked closer to the gate, and then he stopped.

Looking down on him, the first guard said, "Zortan's horde took Artama."

"Zortan and his men are dead."

"Artama is dead. Everyone knows the tale."

Indeed, the tale had become a legend, told and retold in story and song. Volumes had already been written.

The guard added, "Artama would be older."

"But you see I did not die."

"What do I see? A dirty stranger."

On the gate tower, through a crenel, Artama saw a third guard whisper in the ear of the first guard. Artama called out, "Send for my father."

There was a quiet moment, and then the first guard commanded someone Artama could not see, "Send for Alagon! Send Taladar." And then he shouted, "Open the gate!"

Artama walked forward slowly, and soon he was inside.

There, another guard repeated, "Who are you? And what is your business?"

"I am Artama, and I have returned."

A small crowd was gathering. A boy pushed his way through to the front. He stood listening.

The guard advanced, leveling his spear. "Where have you been?"

"Across The Plain. After Zortan and his men were destroyed by dragon-fire, I found myself across The Plain. I saw Kora again, and I met Thorne. And . . . ." Artama stopped abruptly. He remembered Kora's admonition. Thoughtfully, Artama continued, "I have seen many things . . . but not my death."

Now, Artama had doubts.

The crowd was growing, yet the boy stayed at the front.

Waiting, Artama stood quietly, disheveled and dirty, covered with the dust of The Plain. His face was streaked with sweat. The left sleeve of his shirt was missing. His shoulder was bruised, and through dried blood, a golden glow was seen.

The crowd began to murmur.

"Look at his shoulder."

"What kind of clothes are those?"

"Have you ever seen anything . . . ?"

"What is he carrying on his back?"

"Look at the star on his forehead."

"It glows."

Suddenly, Taladar was driving a horse-drawn cart toward the crowd, dust billowing behind. Seated beside Taladar was Artama's father. As the cart neared, the crowd separated. Taladar drew rein and brought the cart to a stop in front of Artama.

The horse whinnied.

The crowd grew silent.

Taladar helped the old man down from the cart.

Alagon took several unsteady steps forward and squinted at the tattered young man covered with the dust of The Plain.

The guard demanded, "Well?"

The old man turned his back to the guard and faced the crowd and jubilantly proclaimed, "My son has returned! My son is alive!"

Artama ran to his father, and father and son embraced.

The boy at the front of the crowd turned and ran toward his home in the heart of The Town, shouting, "Artama has returned! Artama is back from the dead!"

An old woman, sweeping in front of the doorway of her cottage, heard the boy as he ran past. Carrying her broom, she hurried inside, calling to her husband, "Artama is risen! Artama is risen from the dead!"

Alagon held Artama by the shoulders and looked into his eyes. He leaned forward and whispered, "Beware, my son. These are dark times."

52455269R00102

Made in the USA
Columbia, SC
04 March 2019